Percentages Book

by Jerry Pallotta
Illustrated by Rob Bolster

Cartwheel
B·O·O·K·S ®
SCHOLASTIC INC.

New York   Toronto   London   Auckland   Sydney   Mexico City   New Delhi   Hong Kong

Thank you to Andy Pallotta who is twenty-five percent of my brothers.
He is also sixteen point sixty-six percent of my brothers and sisters.

——— *Jerry Pallotta*

This book is dedicated to my art teacher, Tom DelSignore. He always made the art room a fun place to be.

——— *Rob Bolster*

Text copyright © 2001 by Jerry Pallotta.
Illustrations copyright © 2001 by Rob Bolster.
All rights reserved. Published by Scholastic Inc.
SCHOLASTIC, CARTWHEEL BOOKS, and associated logos
are trademarks and/or registered trademarks of Scholastic Inc.

HERSHEY'S OFFICIAL LICENSED PRODUCT

Library of Congress Cataloging-in-Publication Data available

ISBN 0-439-25407-8

10 9 8 7 6 5 4 3 2 1   01 02 03 04 05

Printed in Mexico
This edition first printing, September 2001

This really happened, but no one believes me. On the day our class was going to learn percentages, I noticed a lot of candy on my teacher's desk. I wondered what percentage each of us would get. Then a mini-spaceship started talking. . . .

Earthlings, we have come to visit your planet. If you give us TWIZZLERS® Twists, we will teach you about percentages.

$$\frac{75}{100} = .75 = 75\%$$

FRACTION   DECIMAL   PERCENTAGE

These three equal numbers identify parts of a whole amount.

. . . and here are some math symbols to help you figure out percentages.

This is a division sign. It is used to divide numbers. A fraction is a numerator divided by a denominator. The line between a numerator and a denominator is called a fraction bar and is also considered a division sign.

This is a decimal point.
It is used to separate whole numbers from decimals.

This is a percentage symbol. It is used to show that a number is a percentage of something.
We use percentages in everyday life.

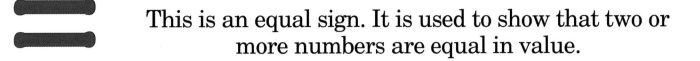 This is an equal sign. It is used to show that two or more numbers are equal in value.

This is a multiplication sign or a times sign. Multiplication is important. To change a decimal to a percentage, you multiply by one hundred.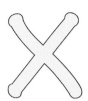

These candies are called TWIZZLERS Twists.

 STRAWBERRY TWIST

LICORICE TWIST

These are our mini-spaceships.
Do not be afraid. We are here to help you.

$$\frac{100}{100} = 1.0 = 100\%$$

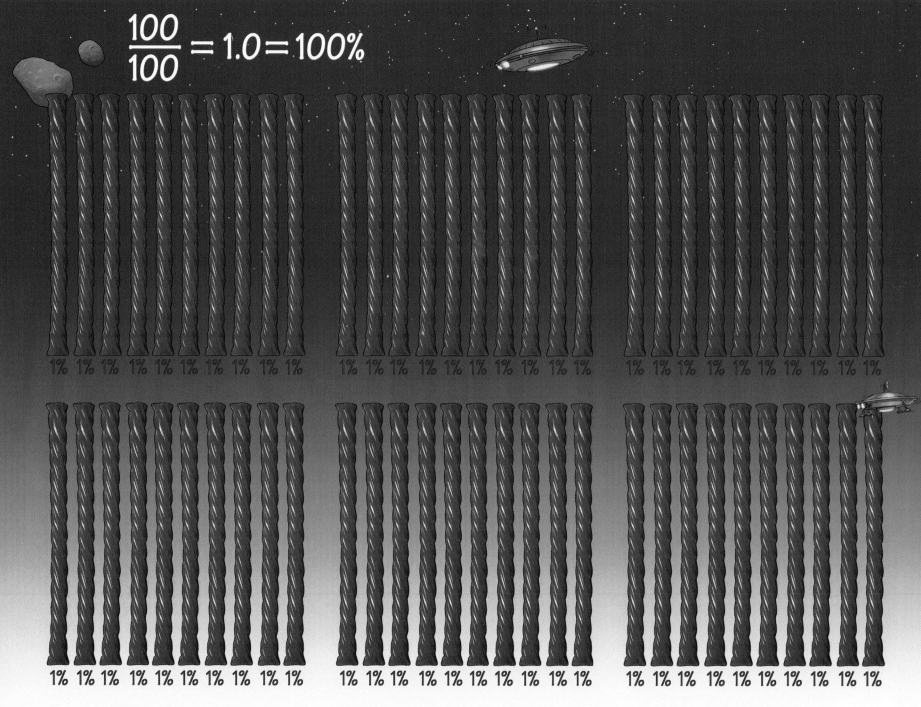

1% 1% 1% 1% 1% 1% 1% 1% 1% 1% 1% 1% 1% 1% 1% 1% 1% 1% 1% 1% 1% 1% 1% 1% 1% 1% 1% 1% 1% 1%

1% 1% 1% 1% 1% 1% 1% 1% 1% 1% 1% 1% 1% 1% 1% 1% 1% 1% 1% 1% 1% 1% 1% 1% 1% 1% 1% 1% 1% 1%

On this page and the next page are one hundred TWIZZLERS Twists.
Percent means "per hundred." One hundred percent is the whole group.

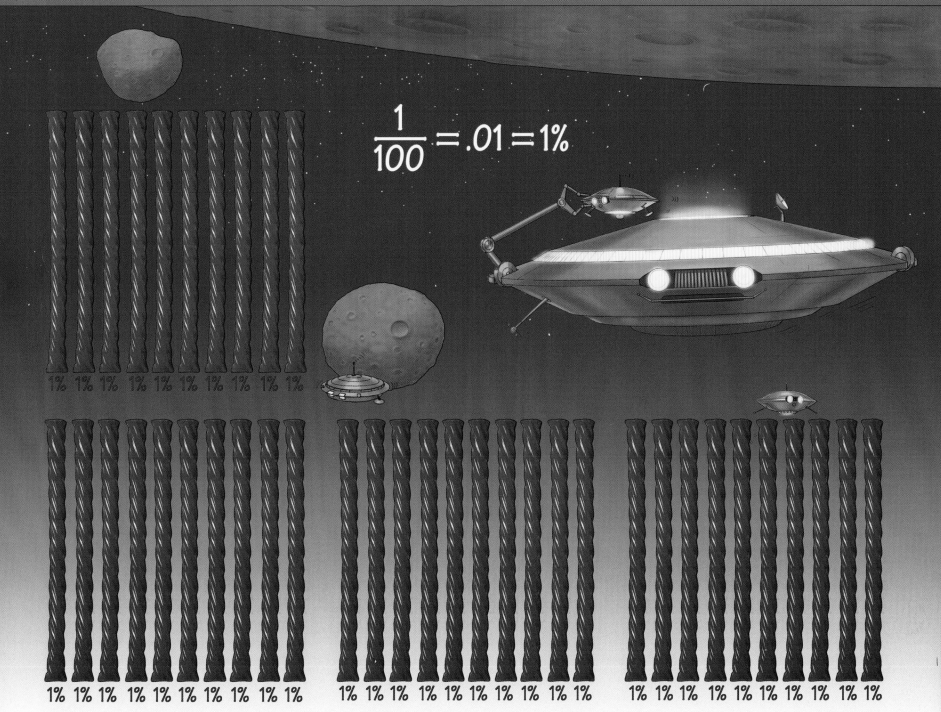

$$\frac{1}{100} = .01 = 1\%$$

1% 1% 1% 1% 1% 1% 1% 1% 1% 1%

1% 1% 1% 1% 1% 1% 1% 1% 1% 1% 1% 1% 1% 1% 1% 1% 1% 1% 1% 1% 1% 1% 1% 1% 1% 1% 1% 1% 1% 1%

Each TWIZZLERS Twist is equal to one percent of this group of one hundred. The fraction, the decimal, and the percentage shown above are equivalent ways of showing the same value.

1 2 3 4 5 6 7 8 9 0

BASE 10

There are hundreds of different alphabets in the galaxy, but almost everyone uses the same number system. You can write any number with the symbols zero, one, two, three, four, five, six, seven, eight, and nine. After nine comes ten, which is really one group of ten and zero ones. It is a base-ten system. Aliens from other planets probably use the same base-ten system.

23.86

It is important to learn place value. Here is a number we picked at random. Twenty-three point eighty-six. This number has two tens, three ones, a decimal point, eight tenths, and six hundredths. The position, or place of a number in relation to the decimal point, determines its place value.

PLACE VALUE

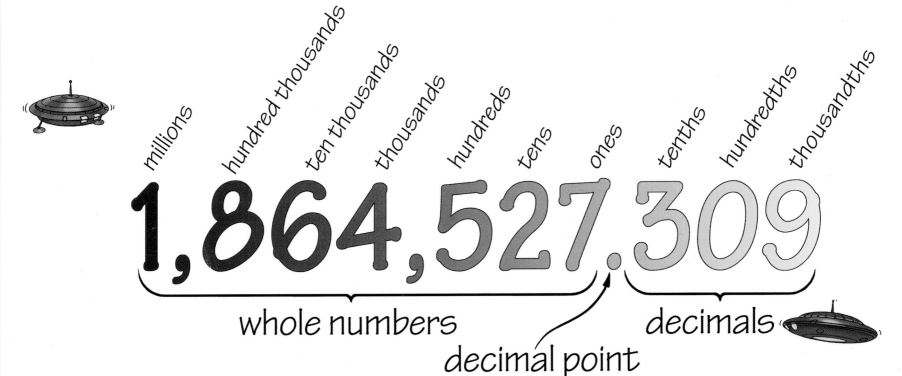

millions — hundred thousands — ten thousands — thousands — hundreds — tens — ones — tenths — hundredths — thousandths

1,864,527.309

whole numbers | decimals

decimal point

Wow! Here is a big number. One million eight hundred sixty-four thousand five hundred twenty-seven point three zero nine.

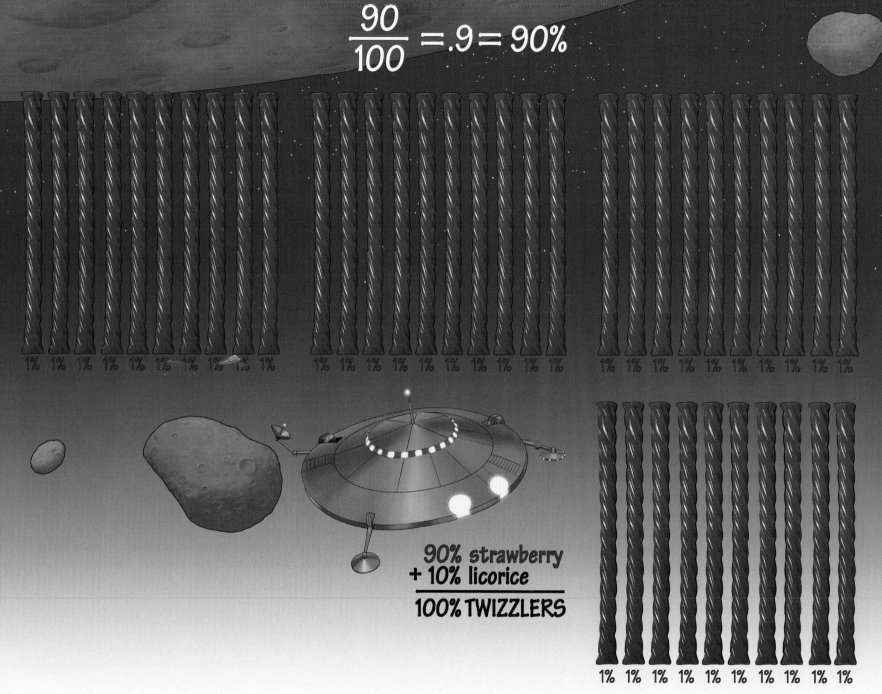

$$\frac{90}{100} = .9 = 90\%$$

90% strawberry
+ 10% licorice
_____
100% TWIZZLERS

Earthlings, notice the difference on these two pages. There are still one hundred TWIZZLERS Twists, but only ninety of them are strawberry-flavored. Ten are licorice-flavored.

$$\frac{10}{100} = .1 = 10\%$$

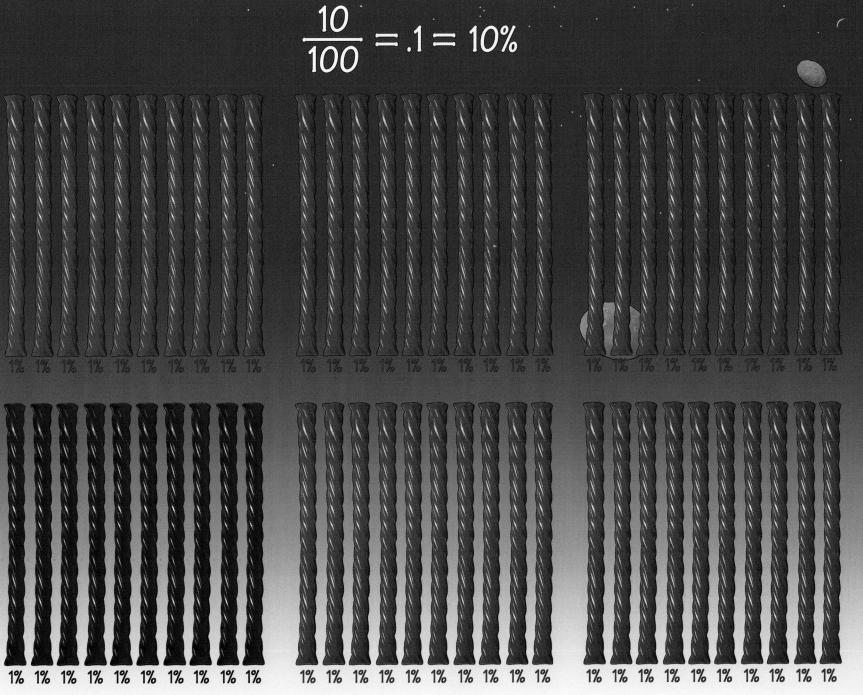

The ninety red ones represent ninety percent. The ten black ones represent ten percent. Ten one-hundredths and point one are also correct ways to show this amount of licorice.

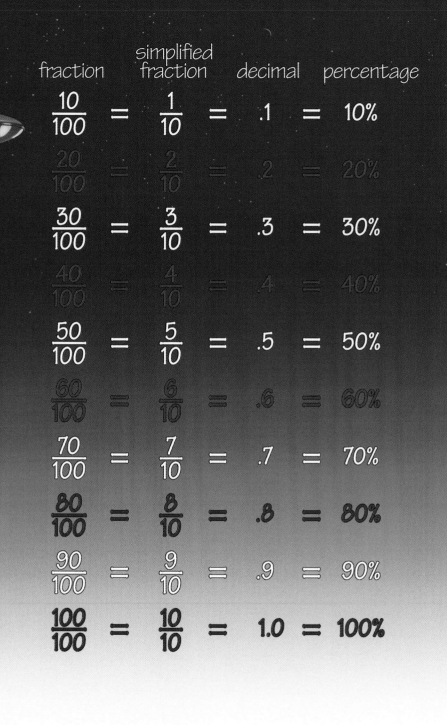

fraction		decimal		percentage
$\frac{1}{100}$	=	.01	=	1%
$\frac{2}{100}$	=	.02	=	2%
$\frac{3}{100}$	=	.03	=	3%
$\frac{4}{100}$	=	.04	=	4%
$\frac{5}{100}$	=	.05	=	5%
$\frac{6}{100}$	=	.06	=	6%
$\frac{7}{100}$	=	.07	=	7%
$\frac{8}{100}$	=	.08	=	8%
$\frac{9}{100}$	=	.09	=	9%
$\frac{10}{100}$	=	.1	=	10%

fraction		simplified fraction		decimal		percentage
$\frac{10}{100}$	=	$\frac{1}{10}$	=	.1	=	10%
$\frac{20}{100}$	=	$\frac{2}{10}$	=	.2	=	20%
$\frac{30}{100}$	=	$\frac{3}{10}$	=	.3	=	30%
$\frac{40}{100}$	=	$\frac{4}{10}$	=	.4	=	40%
$\frac{50}{100}$	=	$\frac{5}{10}$	=	.5	=	50%
$\frac{60}{100}$	=	$\frac{6}{10}$	=	.6	=	60%
$\frac{70}{100}$	=	$\frac{7}{10}$	=	.7	=	70%
$\frac{80}{100}$	=	$\frac{8}{10}$	=	.8	=	80%
$\frac{90}{100}$	=	$\frac{9}{10}$	=	.9	=	90%
$\frac{100}{100}$	=	$\frac{10}{10}$	=	1.0	=	100%

Okay! You get the idea. Do you see any patterns?

Earthlings, here is how to figure out a percentage. Divide the top number of a fraction, the numerator, by the bottom number, the denominator. This will give you a decimal. Move the decimal point two places to the right. Drop the decimal point and add a percent sign.

$\dfrac{1}{10}$ $10\overline{)1}$ $10\overline{)1.0}$ $10\overline{)1.0}$ $\dfrac{10}{0}$ $10\overline{)1.0}$ $\dfrac{10}{0}$ .1   10,   10%

$\dfrac{2}{10}$ $10\overline{)2}$ $10\overline{)2.0}$ $10\overline{)2.0}$ $\dfrac{-20}{0}$ $10\overline{)2.0}$ $\dfrac{-20}{0}$ .2   20,   20%

$\dfrac{39}{100}$ $100\overline{)39}$ $100\overline{)39.0}$ $100\overline{)39.0}$ $\dfrac{-300}{90}$ $100\overline{)39.0}$ $\begin{array}{r}-300\\900\\-900\\\hline 0\end{array}$ .39   39,   39%

$\dfrac{130}{400}$ $400\overline{)130}$ $400\overline{)130.0}$ $\begin{array}{r}-1200\\\hline 100\end{array}$ $400\overline{)130.0}$ $\begin{array}{r}-1200\\1000\\-800\\\hline 2000\\2000\\\hline 0\end{array}$ .325   32,5   32.5%

Try a difficult one.
Don't forget to show your work!

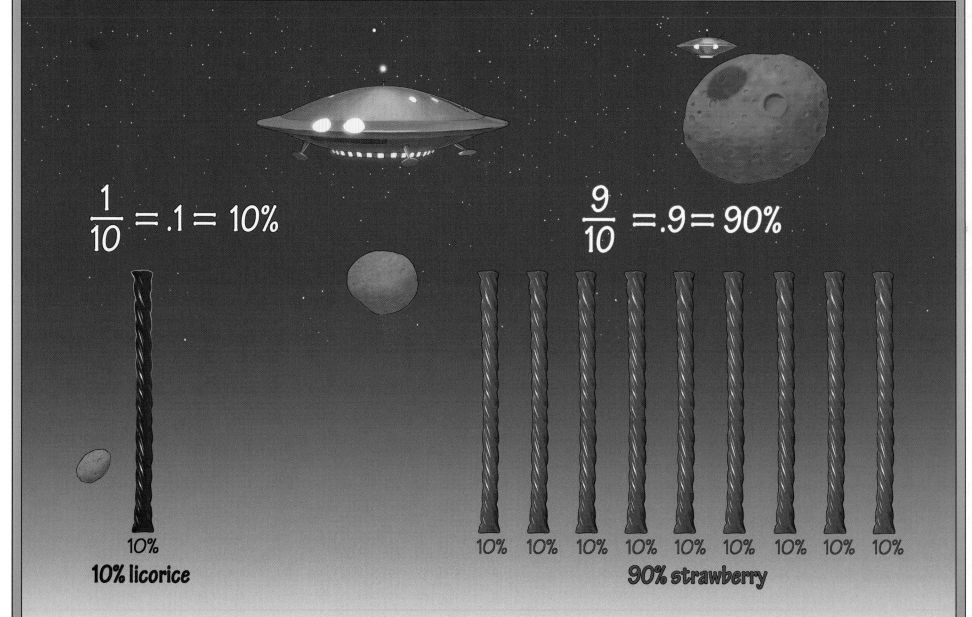

$$\frac{1}{10} = .1 = 10\%$$

$$\frac{9}{10} = .9 = 90\%$$

10%

10% licorice

10% 10% 10% 10% 10% 10% 10% 10% 10%

90% strawberry

90% strawberry
+10% licorice
―――――――――――
100% TWIZZLERS

You do not need a group of one hundred to do percentages. Here are ten TWIZZLERS Twists. In this group, each Twist is equal to ten percent of the total amount. Ten percent are licorice-flavored and ninety percent are strawberry-flavored.

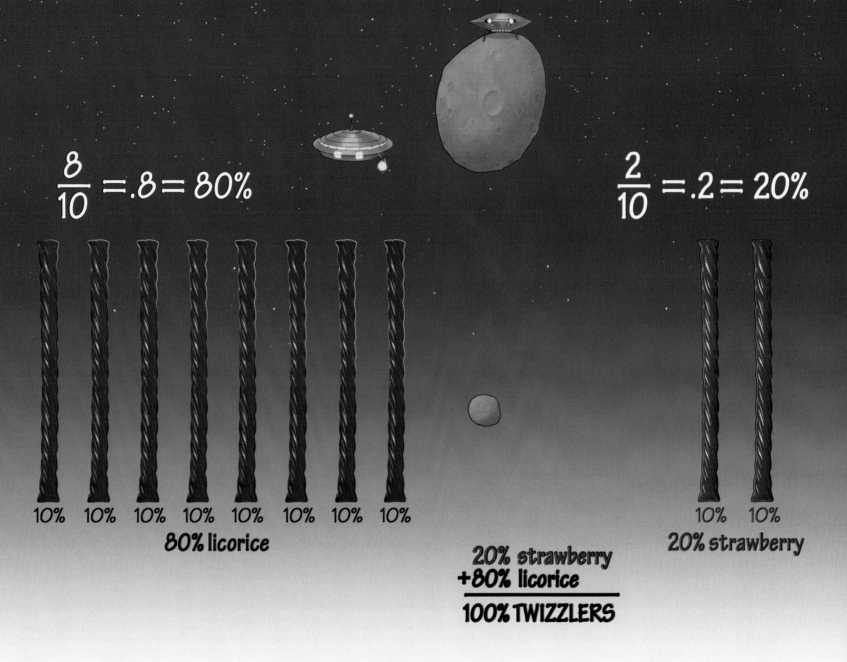

$$\frac{8}{10} = .8 = 80\%$$

$$\frac{2}{10} = .2 = 20\%$$

10% 10% 10% 10% 10% 10% 10% 10%

80% licorice

10% 10%

20% strawberry

20% strawberry
+80% licorice
——————————
100% TWIZZLERS

Here is another group of ten TWIZZLERS Twists. Flavors and colors can change but the math stays the same. Each piece is equal to ten percent. Eighty percent are black and twenty percent are red.

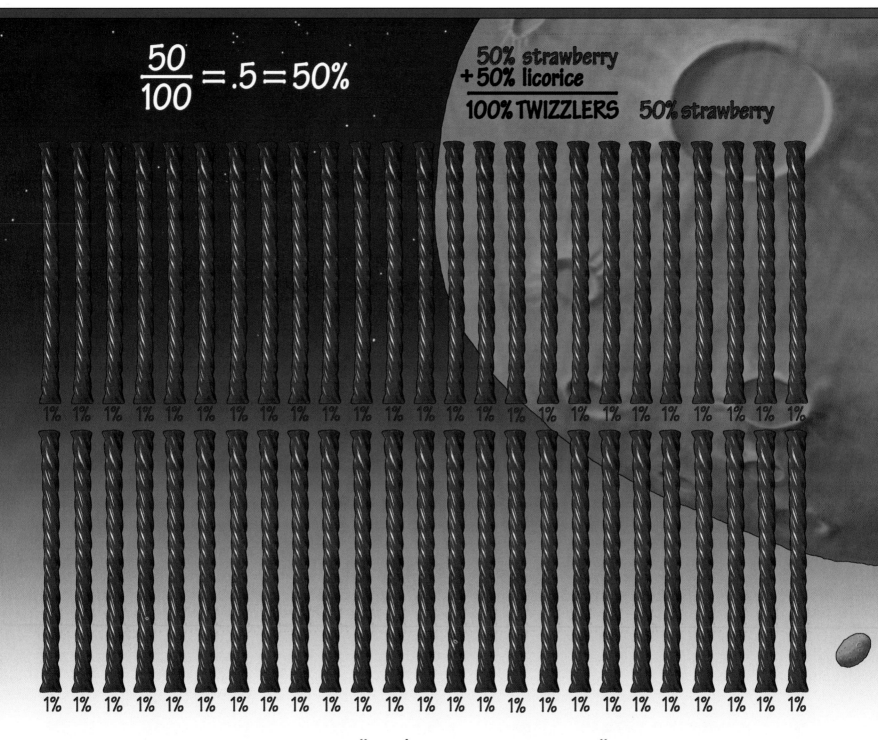

$$\frac{50}{100} = .5 = 50\%$$

50% strawberry
+ 50% licorice
_____
100% TWIZZLERS   50% strawberry

1% 1% 1% 1% 1% 1% 1% 1% 1% 1% 1% 1% 1% 1% 1% 1% 1% 1% 1% 1% 1% 1% 1% 1% 1%

1% 1% 1% 1% 1% 1% 1% 1% 1% 1% 1% 1% 1% 1% 1% 1% 1% 1% 1% 1% 1% 1% 1% 1% 1%

Have you heard someone say, "Let's split it fifty-fifty"? It means each of you gets fifty percent. It also means each of you gets one-half.

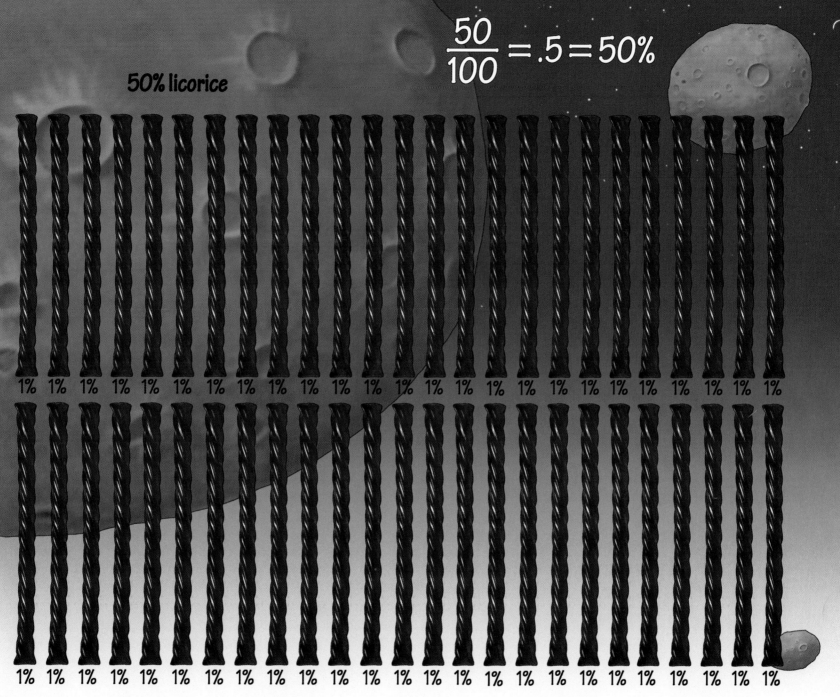

50% licorice

$$\frac{50}{100} = .5 = 50\%$$

1% 1% 1% 1% 1% 1% 1% 1% 1% 1% 1% 1% 1% 1% 1% 1% 1% 1% 1% 1% 1% 1% 1% 1% 1%

1% 1% 1% 1% 1% 1% 1% 1% 1% 1% 1% 1% 1% 1% 1% 1% 1% 1% 1% 1% 1% 1% 1% 1% 1%

How about fifty licorice Twists for you Earthlings and fifty strawberry for us.
We love the red ones. Fifty-fifty! One-half and one-half! Think of other
ways to divide this group "fifty-fifty."

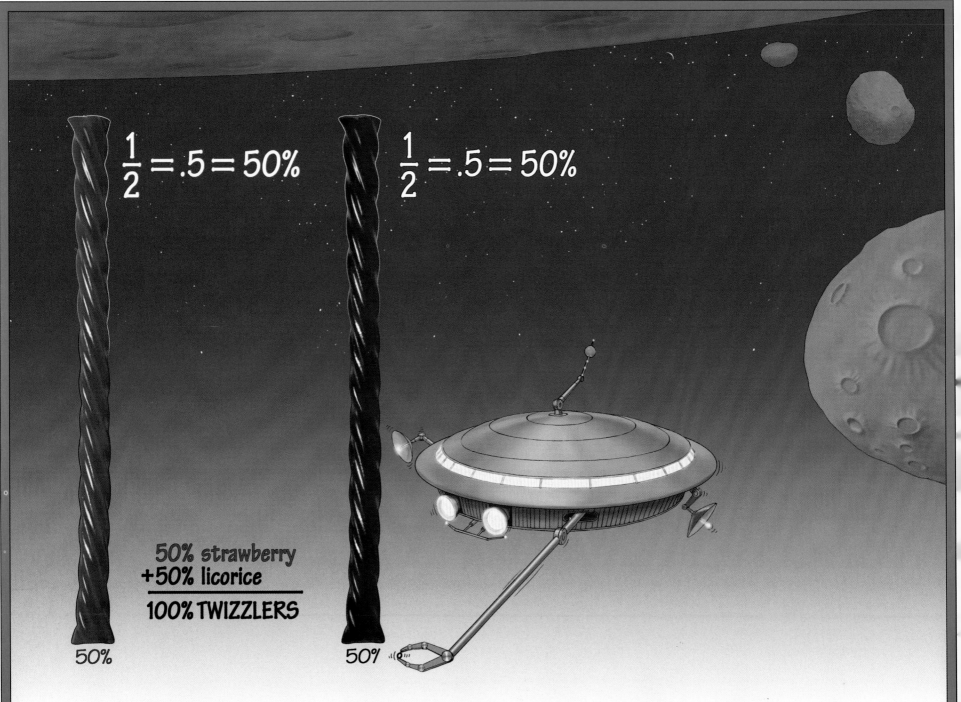

$$\frac{1}{2} = .5 = 50\%$$

$$\frac{1}{2} = .5 = 50\%$$

50% strawberry
+50% licorice
——————
100% TWIZZLERS

50%

50%

If there are only two TWIZZLERS Twists, each Twist is fifty percent of the total amount on this page. You can always figure out "fifty-fifty" by dividing by two. What is your favorite flavor?

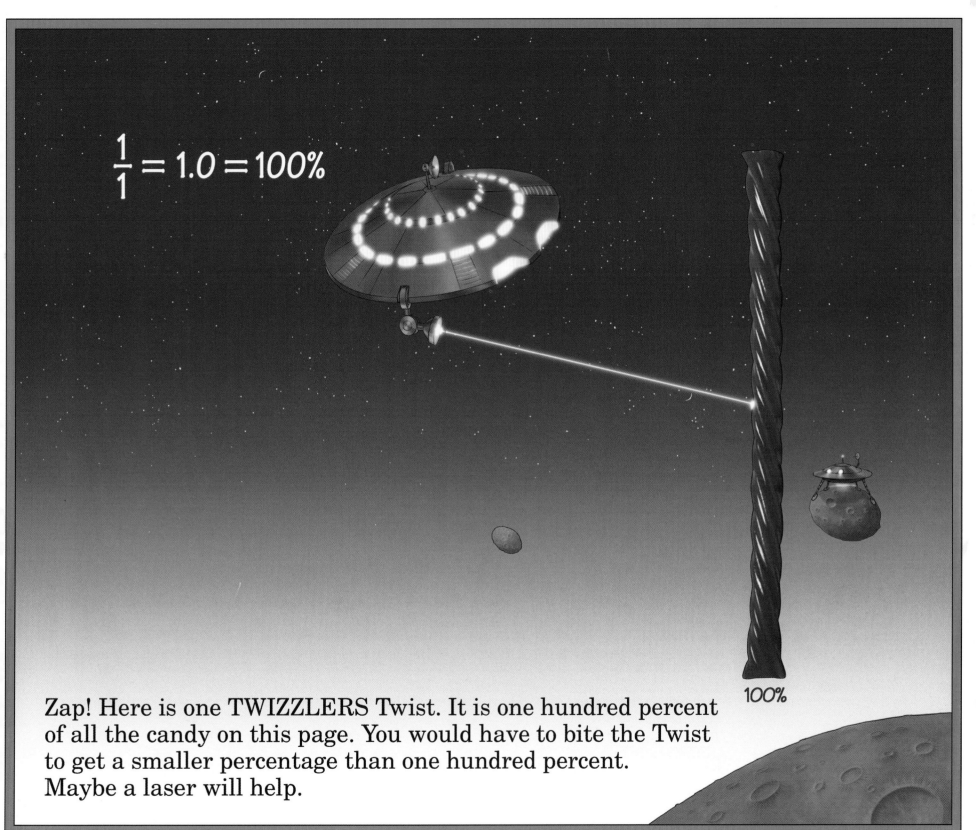

$\dfrac{1}{1} = 1.0 = 100\%$

100%

Zap! Here is one TWIZZLERS Twist. It is one hundred percent of all the candy on this page. You would have to bite the Twist to get a smaller percentage than one hundred percent. Maybe a laser will help.

I'm glad we are learning percentages. Yesterday while walking to school, some of my classmates found ten thousand dollars on the street! Wow!

The police said our class could keep eight percent of the money as a reward. $\$10,000. \times .08 = \$800.$ Eight cents out of every dollar.

The principal of our school hoped we would keep nine percent. $\$10,000. \times .09 = \$900.$ Nine cents per dollar.

The insurance company approved a payment to our class for ten percent. $\$10,000. \times .1 = \$1,000.$ Ten cents per dollar.

The judge at the local courthouse ruled we could keep twelve percent. $\$10,000. \times .12 = \$1,200.$ Twelve cents per dollar.

But luckily the owners of the money came forward. They thanked our class, and we were rewarded with fifteen percent. Yeah! $\$10,000. \times .15 = \$1,500.$ Fifteen cents per dollar.

$$\begin{array}{r} \$10,000. \\ \times .08 \\ \hline \$800.00 \end{array}$$

$$\begin{array}{r} \$10,000. \\ \times .09 \\ \hline \$900.00 \end{array}$$

$$\begin{array}{r} \$10,000. \\ \times .10 \\ \hline 00\,000 \\ 10\,00 \\ \hline \$1,000.00 \end{array}$$

$$\begin{array}{r} \$10,000. \\ \times .12 \\ \hline 20000 \\ 10000 \\ \hline \$1,200.00 \end{array}$$

$$\begin{array}{r} \$10,000. \\ \times .15 \\ \hline 500\,00 \\ 10\,00\,0 \\ \hline \$1,500.00 \end{array}$$

$$\frac{49}{50} = .98 = 98\%$$

$$\frac{1}{50} = .02 = 2\%$$

2% 2% 2% 2% 2%   2% 2% 2% 2% 2%   2% 2% 2% 2% 2%   2% 2% 2% 2% 2%   2% 2% 2% 2% 2%

2% 2% 2% 2% 2%   2% 2% 2% 2% 2%   2% 2% 2% 2% 2%   2% 2% 2% 2% 2%   2% 2% 2% 2% 2%

98% licorice
+2% strawberry
100% TWIZZLERS

In this group of fifty, each Twist is equal to two percent of the total. Ninety-eight percent are black and two percent are red. Watch out for meteors and asteroids.

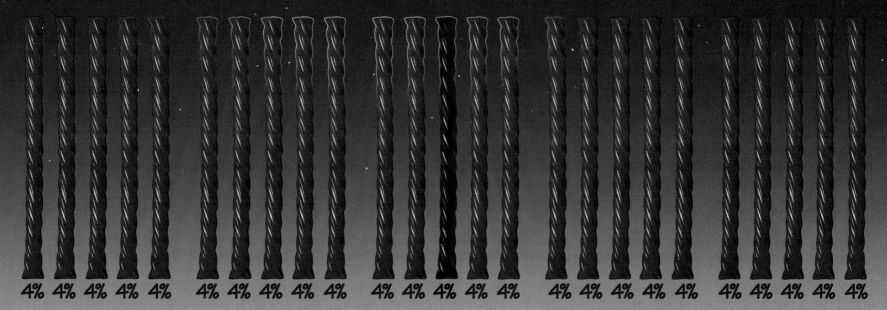

$$\frac{24}{25} = .96 = 96\%$$

$$\frac{1}{25} = .04 = 4\%$$

4% 4% 4% 4% 4% 4% 4% 4% 4% 4% 4% 4% 4% 4% 4% 4% 4% 4% 4% 4% 4% 4% 4% 4% 4%

$$\frac{\begin{array}{r} 4\% \text{ licorice} \\ +96\% \text{ strawberry} \end{array}}{100\% \text{ TWIZZLERS}}$$

In another area, there are twenty-five Twists.
Twenty-four are strawberry-flavored and one is licorice-flavored.
What percent of the total is each piece of candy? Think about it and do the math.

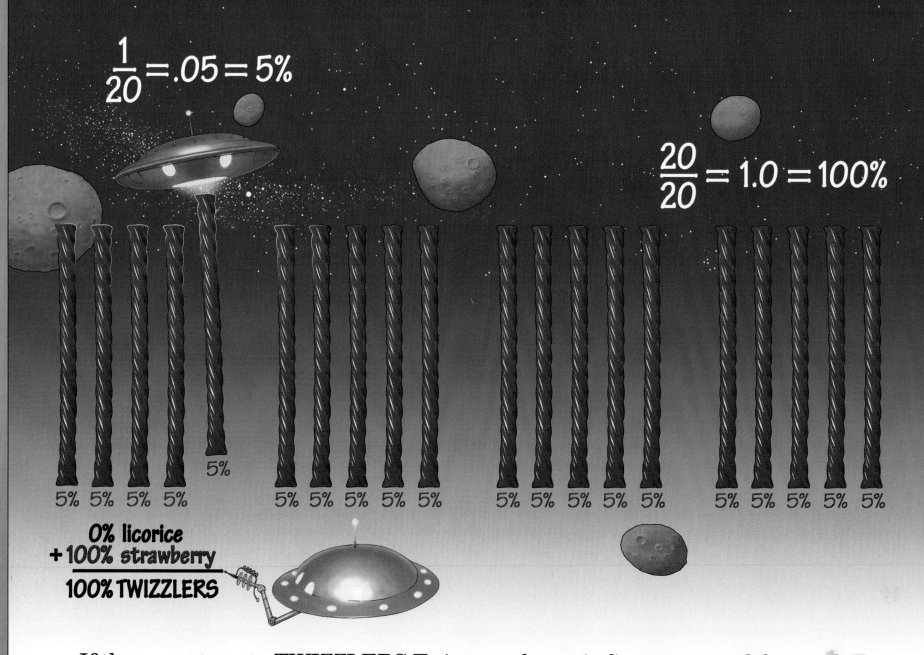

$$\frac{1}{20} = .05 = 5\%$$

$$\frac{20}{20} = 1.0 = 100\%$$

5%

5% 5% 5% 5%   5% 5% 5% 5% 5%   5% 5% 5% 5% 5%   5% 5% 5% 5% 5%

0% licorice
+ 100% strawberry
─────────────
100% TWIZZLERS

If there are twenty TWIZZLERS Twists, each one is five percent of the total. Two would be ten percent, three would be fifteen percent. You can add them if you want to. All of them added together equal one hundred percent, but you know that.

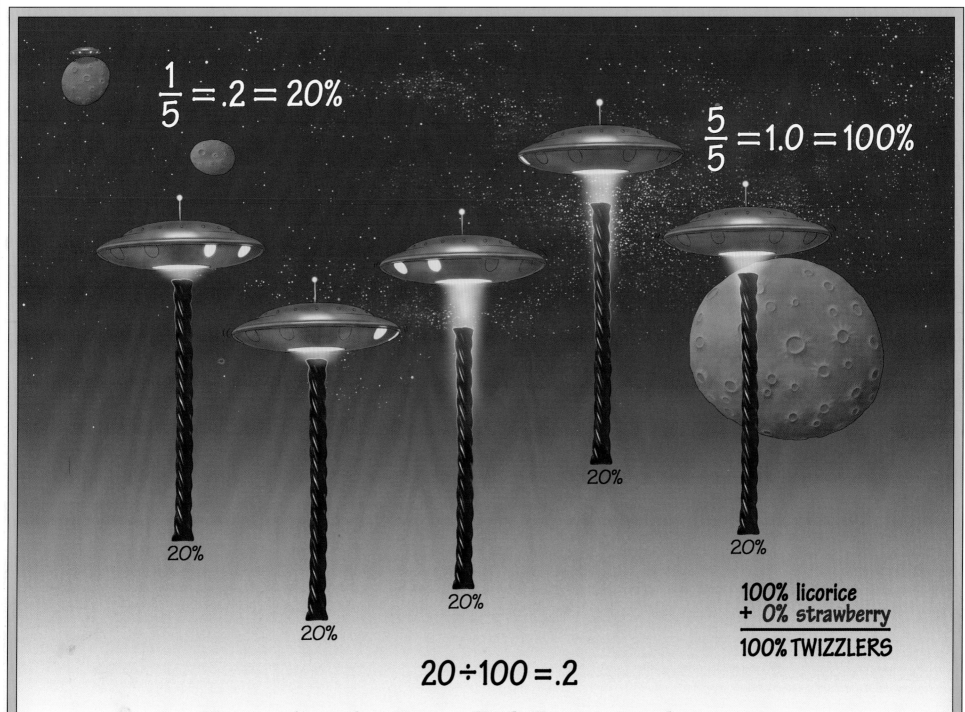

$$\frac{1}{5} = .2 = 20\%$$

$$\frac{5}{5} = 1.0 = 100\%$$

20%

20%

20%

20%

20%

100% licorice
+ 0% strawberry

100% TWIZZLERS

$$20 \div 100 = .2$$

Here we have five Twists. Each Twist is equal to twenty
percent. To change a percent to a fraction, drop the percent sign and divide
by one hundred. Oops, we are back to a decimal.

AVG	SLG	AB	H	S	2B	3B	HR	BB	OBP
.325	.595	400	130	78	22	4	26	100	.460

.325

A famous Earthling finished the baseball season with a batting average of three-twenty-five! A batting average is a percentage. It is calculated by dividing the number of "hits" by the number of "at bats."

H ÷ AB = AVG

130 ÷ 400 = .325

.595

The SLG, or "slugging percentage," is calculated by adding singles as ones, doubles as twos, triples as threes, and home runs as fours. This number is divided by the total number of "at bats."

$$78 + 44 + 12 + 104 = 238$$

$$238 \div 400 = .595$$

.460

The OBP, or "on-base percentage," is calculated by adding walks plus hits divided by walks plus "at bats."

$$BB + H \div BB + AB = OBP$$

$$100 + 130 \div 100 + 400 = .460$$

When watching or playing baseball, you are doing math!

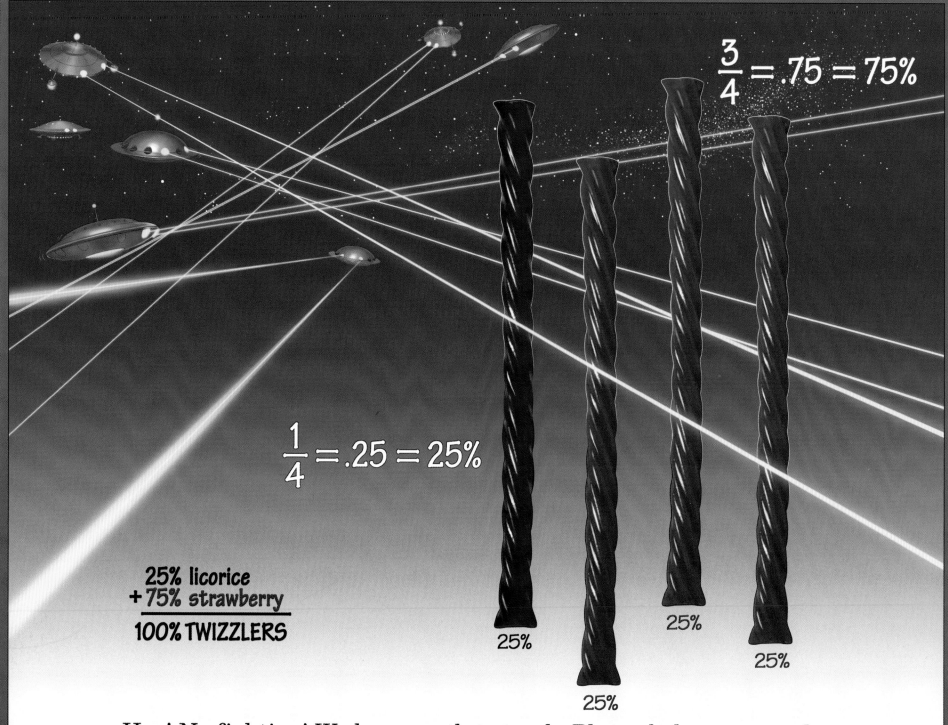

$$\frac{3}{4} = .75 = 75\%$$

$$\frac{1}{4} = .25 = 25\%$$

25% licorice
+75% strawberry
100% TWIZZLERS

25%

25%

25%

25%

Hey! No fighting! We have math to teach. Please behave yourselves,
you other aliens. Terminate those lasers!

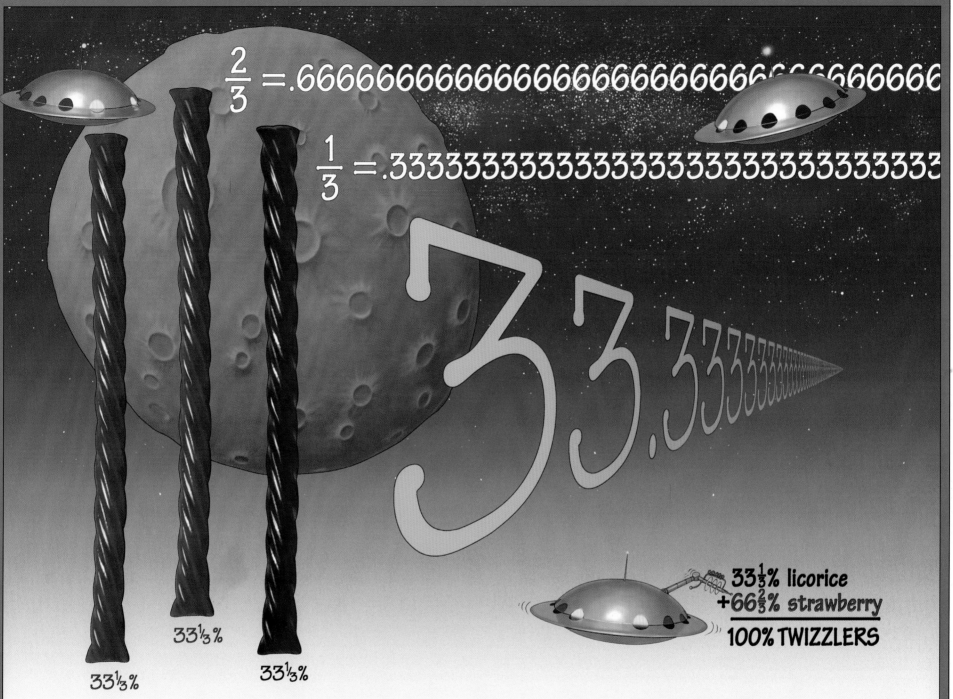

$$\frac{2}{3} = .66666666666666666666666666666666666$$

$$\frac{1}{3} = .33333333333333333333333333333333333$$

33.3333333333

33⅓% licorice
+66⅔% strawberry
_____
100% TWIZZLERS

33⅓%

33⅓%

33⅓%

Not all decimals are easy to understand. Here are three TWIZZLERS Twists. Each one is equal to thirty-three point three three three three three three three three three three three and it keeps going on forever. It is enough to drive you nuts.

Earthlings, there are nine planets in your solar system. Mercury, Venus, Earth, Mars, Jupiter, Saturn, Uranus, Neptune, and Pluto. The red strawberry one is our favorite.

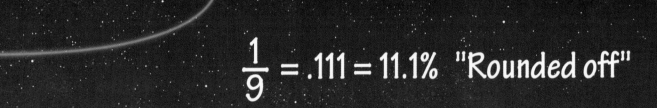

$$\frac{1}{9} = .111 = 11.1\% \quad \textit{"Rounded off"}$$

Do you know how many planets in your solar system have life? We are not sure either, but the answer may be one-ninth. One-ninth is equal to eleven point one percent rounded off. We would teach you about "rounding off" non-terminating decimals but it is time for us to go.

There are twenty-five kids in my class. Now that we all know percentages, we can do the math. We each get eight TWIZZLERS Twists. Four percent of the total. Twenty-five percent of the eight are licorice. Seventy-five percent are strawberry. That's it! Two licorice and six strawberry each. That's a ratio of two to six! Our teacher says we will learn about ratios next week. Mini-spaceships, please come back!

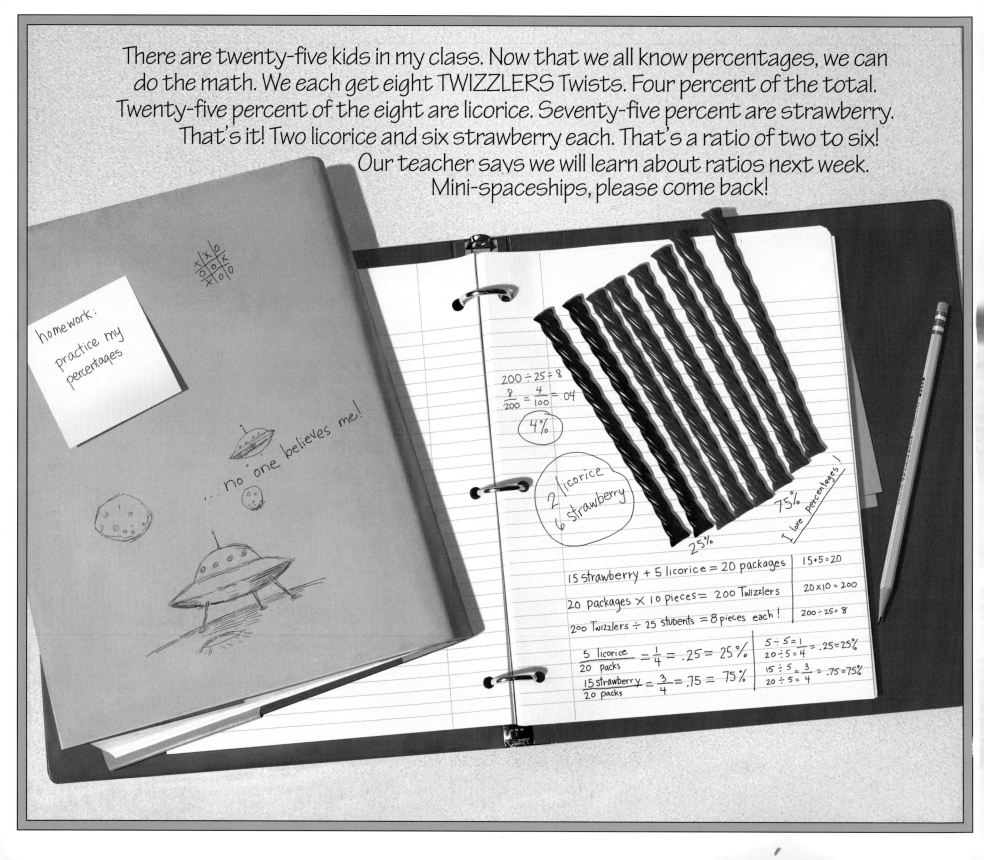

homework: practice my percentages

...no one believes me!

$200 \div 25 = 8$

$\frac{8}{200} = \frac{4}{100} = .04$

4%

2 licorice
6 strawberry

25%

75%

I love percentages!

15 strawberry + 5 licorice = 20 packages	15 + 5 = 20
20 packages × 10 pieces = 200 Twizzlers	20 × 10 = 200
200 Twizzlers ÷ 25 students = 8 pieces each!	200 ÷ 25 = 8
$\frac{5 \text{ licorice}}{20 \text{ packs}} = \frac{1}{4} = .25 = 25\%$	$\frac{5 \div 5 = 1}{20 \div 5 = 4} = .25 = 25\%$
$\frac{15 \text{ strawberry}}{20 \text{ packs}} = \frac{3}{4} = .75 = 75\%$	$\frac{15 \div 5 = 3}{20 \div 5 = 4} = .75 = 75\%$

Zeus

by Nancy Loewen

Consultant:
Kenneth F. Kitchell Jr., Ph.D.
Department of Classics
University of Massachusetts, Amherst

RiverFront Books

an imprint of Franklin Watts
A Division of Grolier Publishing
New York   London   Hong Kong   Sydney
Danbury, Connecticut

RiverFront Books
http://publishing.grolier.com

Library of Congress Cataloging-in-Publication Data
Loewen, Nancy, 1964–
    Zeus/by Nancy Loewen.
    p. cm.—(Greek and Roman mythology)
    Includes bibliographical references and index.
    Summary: Surveys classical mythology, discussing the relationship between
Greek and Roman myths, and describes the life and exploits of the god Zeus.
    ISBN 0-7368-0051-4
    1. Zeus (Greek deity)—Juvenile literature. [1. Zeus (Greek deity)
2. Mythology, Greek. 3. Mythology, Roman.] I. Title. II. Series.
BL820.J8L64   1999
292.2'113—dc21
                                                                98-35112
                                                                     CIP
                                                                      AC

Editorial Credits
Christy Steele, editor; Clay Schotzko/Icon Productions, cover designer;
    Timothy Halldin, illustrator; Sheri Gosewisch, photo researcher

Photo Credits
Archive Photos, 17, 34, 39
Art Resource, cover; Fratelli Alinari, 4; Scala, 18, 20, 24, 26, 28, 37, 43
Corbis-Bettmann, 11, 31, 32
Unicorn Stock Photos/Bob Barrett, 14
Visuals Unlimited, 40; Charles W. McRae, 22

Table of Contents

This book is illustrated with photographs of statues, paintings, illustrations, and other artwork about mythology by artists from both ancient and modern times.

Chapter One

About Mythology

As early as 2000 B.C., Greek and Roman people used stories to help them understand the world. These stories served important purposes. Most people did not know much about science. So they used their stories to explain human history and the natural world.

The stories created a sense of order in the lives of ancient Greeks and Romans. The stories featured characters people could understand to make the world seem more familiar and less frightening.

Greek and Roman people believed that gods, goddesses, heroes, and monsters controlled the world. These powerful beings were the main characters in the stories ancient people told.

Scholars today call these stories myths. The collection of the hundreds of Greek and Roman

People believed that goddesses, heroes, monsters, and gods such as Zeus controlled the world.

myths is called classical mythology. People no longer believe that myths are true. Instead, they rely on science to explain the world. Greeks and Romans told several types of myths.

Explanation myths tell how things happen. According to one Greek myth, a huge bull that lived underground caused earthquakes. Other myths explained the groupings of the stars in the sky and the change in seasons.

Characters search for something in quest myths. The search may be for treasure or for a person. Heroes usually are the main characters in quest myths. Heroes must face dangers and hardships to complete their quests. Their strength, bravery, and intelligence help them succeed. Quest myths teach people values. From the myths, people learn to keep trying to accomplish their goals, even during hard times.

History of Mythology

The stories in classical mythology started in both ancient Greece and Rome. Greece is a country in what is now Europe. The Roman Empire was a group of countries under Roman

rule. Rome was the capital city of the Roman Empire. Rome is in what is now Italy.

Greeks were among the first people to tell stories about gods, goddesses, heroes, and monsters. They began telling these myths in about 2000 B.C. Greek people told their stories to new generations.

The Roman Empire conquered Greece in about 100 B.C. The Roman people liked Greek myths. Romans began to tell stories about

Gods and Goddesses
of Greek and Roman Mythology

Zeus (Greek)   Jupiter (Roman)
King of the gods and goddesses

Hera (Greek)   Juno (Roman)
Queen of the gods and goddesses

Athena (Greek)   Minerva (Roman)
Goddess of wisdom and war

Apollo (Greek)   No Roman Name
God of beauty, the Sun, prophecy, and healing

Artemis (Greek)   Diana (Roman)
Goddess of the moon and the hunt

Hermes (Greek)   Mercury (Roman)
God of business and commerce; messenger to Zeus

Aphrodite (Greek)   Venus (Roman)
Goddess of love, beauty, and fertility

Dionysus (Greek)   Bacchus (Roman)
God of wine, song, and drama

Poseidon (Greek)   Neptune (Roman)
God of the seas

Hades (Greek)   Pluto (Roman)
God of the Underworld

Demeter (Greek)   Ceres (Roman)
Goddess of agriculture

Ares (Greek)   Mars (Roman)
God of war

Hephaestus (Greek)   Vulcan (Roman)
God of fire

Hestia (Greek)   Vesta (Roman)
Goddess of the hearth

Greek characters. Some of the Roman stories were the same as Greek stories. Romans gave the characters new names. For example, the Greek king of the gods was called Zeus. The Roman king of the gods was called Jupiter. Both Zeus and Jupiter had the same powers and duties. This book uses the Greek names of the mythological characters.

Storytellers memorized myths and told the stories to people. Many ancient Greeks and Romans did not know how to write and read. They could not write the myths down on paper. Instead, people learned the myths from the storytellers.

Storytellers sometimes added new ideas to make the myths seem more exciting. Some storytellers told the myths incorrectly. Many versions of the myths exist today because storytellers told the myths in different ways.

The First Gods

Chaos gave birth to the oldest god, Heaven, and the oldest goddess, Earth. Heaven and Earth had many children. Some of their children had 150 hands. Earth also gave birth to cyclopes. These giants had only one eye in the middle of their foreheads. Earth also gave birth to several powerful giants called titans.

Heaven was cruel. He did not like the 150-handed giants or the cyclopes. So he locked these children underground. Heaven let the titans remain free.

Heaven's son, Cronus, was a titan. Cronus did not like how his father ruled. Cronus wanted to rule the world. So he defeated his father and became the ruler.

Cronus was an evil ruler like his father. He kept the cyclopes and the 150-handed giants locked underground. He locked Heaven underground too. This made his mother, Earth, angry.

Other Gods and Goddesses

Some gods and goddesses were more powerful than others. The gods and goddesses sometimes fought each other to increase their power and rank. Zeus became the most powerful god. He was Cronus' son.

People believed the powerful gods and goddesses lived on top of Mount Olympus.

Zeus became the most powerful god.

Mount Olympus is the highest mountain in Greece. The powerful beings on Mount Olympus became known as the Olympians. Zeus lived in a palace on Mount Olympus. Less important gods and goddesses lived throughout the earth, sky, and sea.

The gods and goddesses behaved very much like humans. Zeus was usually calm and fair. He punished criminals and helped people who were honest and sincere. He often settled fights between the other gods.

But unlike humans, Zeus and other gods and goddesses had magic powers that were almost unlimited. He could turn himself and others into different shapes. Zeus could create storms, objects, people, and monsters. He was immortal. Zeus would never die.

Religion

Greeks and Romans worshiped the gods and goddesses from their stories. Each person worshiped the powerful beings that mattered most to their lives. People who needed justice prayed to Zeus for help.

Greeks and Romans honored the gods and goddesses in many ways. Some built temples to honor their favorite gods or goddesses. People brought offerings of money and food to the temples. Artists painted pictures and made statues of the gods and goddesses. Some of the artwork decorated the temples.

Characters in Mythology

Classical mythology contained hundreds of characters. Some characters appeared in many different stories. Other were in only a few myths. Most characters belonged to one of the following groups:

Titans: These gods and goddesses were powerful giants. They were the children of Earth and Heaven.

Olympians: These were the main gods in classical mythology. Olympians looked like humans. But they had magic powers. They ruled from the top of Mount Olympus. Zeus was the head of the Olympians.

Lesser gods: These gods were less powerful than the Olympians. They often were associated with one particular area such as a river or mountain.

Demigods: These were half-god and half-human characters. They had more power than ordinary humans, but were weaker than the gods. Demigods were not immortal.

Monsters: Monsters could be a combination of different animals or of animals and humans. Gods sent monsters to punish people.

Chapter Two

Young Zeus

Zeus is a character in many myths from classical mythology. Some stories tell how Zeus became the ruler of the world and the head of the gods and goddesses.

Most myths feature Zeus' weapons. He used thunder, lightning bolts, and storms to fight. Zeus trained an eagle to retrieve the lightning bolts he threw at objects.

Birth of Zeus

Cronus married his titan sister, Rhea. Rhea gave birth to several children. Cronus and Rhea's children were Olympians. They looked like humans but they were gods and goddesses.

Cronus did not want his children to conquer him. He ate all of his first five children right

Zeus' weapons were thunder, lightning bolts, and storms.

after they were born. The children lived but were trapped inside Cronus' body.

Rhea was mad that Cronus ate their children. She decided to trick Cronus the next time she had a child. Rhea gave birth to their sixth child, Zeus. Cronus asked for Zeus. Instead, Rhea gave Cronus a stone wrapped in a blanket. Cronus thought the stone was the baby, Zeus. He swallowed the stone.

Rhea hid Zeus from his father. She sent Zeus to a distant island. Nymphs cared for the young Zeus. A nymph is a female goddess who lives in forests, meadows, mountains, or streams. The nymphs fed Zeus goat's milk and honey.

The nymphs sang and played musical instruments when Zeus cried. This covered the noise of the crying. The nymphs did not want Cronus to hear the baby. Otherwise Cronus might realize Rhea had tricked him.

Zeus grew up to be healthy and strong. He wanted to conquer his father. But he knew he could not fight his father by himself. He needed the help of his brothers and sisters.

Cronus ate five of his children right after they were born.

Rescue

Zeus asked Metis for help. Metis was a titan who was the early goddess of wisdom. Metis gave Zeus a magic liquid that would save his brothers and sisters.

Zeus had to get Cronus to drink the magic liquid. So he disguised himself and gave the liquid to Cronus. Cronus drank the liquid and began to choke. He coughed so hard that his five children fell out of his mouth. Demeter, Hestia, and Hera were Cronus' daughters. Poseidon and Hades were his sons.

Battle for Power

Cronus did not want to let the Olympians remain free. So Zeus and his brothers and sisters joined forces to fight Cronus. Zeus wanted to rule the world.

Most of the other titans wanted their brother, Cronus, to remain the ruler. Cronus led these giant gods and goddesses in battles against the Olympians. The war went on for 10 years.

Zeus grew up to be healthy and strong.

Finally, Earth supported Zeus. She was angry because Cronus had not let the 150-handed giants and the cyclopes free. She told Zeus to set the 150-handed giants and the cyclopes free. Zeus did as she wished.

The giants and the cyclopes were grateful to Zeus. They gave Zeus and the Olympians powerful gifts to help them fight against the titans. The cyclopes gave Zeus weapons of thunder and lightning. They gave Hades a helmet that made him invisible. The cyclopes gave Poseidon a magic, three-pointed spear called a trident. The earth shook and the sea became stormy when he struck the ground with his trident.

The titans were frightened of the powerful weapons. So they decided to surrender. Zeus wanted to punish the titans for the long war. He locked them underground. The 150-handed giants guarded the titans. Zeus had a special punishment for the strongest titan, Atlas. Zeus made Atlas hold up the heavens on his shoulders.

Zeus set the cyclopes free.

Zeus trapped Typhon beneath Mount Etna.

Typhon

Zeus conquered Cronus and the titans. But his fight was not finished. Earth became angry with Zeus. She did not want him to lock the titans underground. She wanted all of her children to be free. So Earth decided to punish Zeus.

Earth sent a horrible monster, Typhon, to kill Zeus. Typhon was as tall as a mountain. Flames shot out of his eyes. Snakes circled the lower part of his body. Wings grew out of his back. He had dragons' heads on his hands instead of fingers.

Typhon frightened the Olympians. All but Zeus turned themselves into animals to hide from Typhon. Zeus had to fight Typhon alone.

Zeus and Typhon fought for a long time. Zeus threw lightning bolts at Typhon. Typhon threw mountains at Zeus.

Zeus finally trapped Typhon beneath Mount Etna. This mountain was so large and strong it could hold Typhon forever. Typhon sent flames and smoke out of Mount Etna's top. The ancient Greeks told this myth to explain how Mount Etna became a volcano.

Zeus' victory made him the king of all the gods. He shared his power with his brothers. They divided the world. Poseidon became the ruler of the seas. Hades became the ruler of the dead in the Underworld. Zeus became the ruler of the heavens.

Chapter Three

Children of Zeus

Zeus married Metis after he won the war against the titans. For a while, he and Metis had a happy life on Mount Olympus.

But Zeus' mother, Rhea, warned Zeus. She said that one day Zeus and Metis would have a son. Rhea said that Metis' son would grow up and conquer Zeus.

Zeus did not want to be conquered. He did not want Metis to have a son. Zeus swallowed Metis to be safe. Metis was trapped inside Zeus forever.

Hera

Zeus married his sister Hera after he swallowed his first wife, Metis. But Zeus was not faithful to Hera. He often fell in love with other goddesses and human women.

Zeus married Hera.

Zeus was too powerful for Hera to punish.

Hera often became angry at Zeus and those he loved. But Zeus was too powerful for her to punish. So she punished the women who had Zeus' children instead.

This did not stop Zeus from falling in love with other people. He disguised himself when

26

he saw other women. He made himself look like animals. He did not want Hera to see him in love with other women.

Zeus had many famous children. Some were half-human and half-god children called demigods. Children he had with other goddesses were full gods or goddesses. Classical mythology includes many stories about how these children came into the world.

Europa

Europa was the beautiful daughter of a king. One day, she was playing with some girls on a beach. A strange bull wandered near them. The bull was white and gentle. The girls gathered around the bull. They petted the bull. Europa even climbed on the bull's back.

The bull walked to the ocean with Europa on its back. It did not stop when it came to the water. It went into the water and began to swim.

Europa realized that the bull was really a god. Zeus had used his powers to make himself look like a bull. He took Europa to the island of Crete. Zeus changed back into his usual form on the island.

Perseus cut off Medusa's head and gave it to Athena.

Europa stayed on Crete for the rest of her life. She and Zeus had three sons. The sons became judges in the Underworld.

Danae

Zeus also fell in love with Danae. An oracle told Danae's father that Danae would give birth to a son. Priests or priestesses served as oracles. The gods talked through them. The oracle said that Danae's son would grow up and kill his grandfather.

Danae's father did not want this to happen. He locked Danae in an underground room and did not let any men visit her.

Zeus tricked Danae's father. Zeus used his powers to make himself look like a shower of gold. The gold rained down on Danae. She became pregnant. She gave birth to the hero Perseus.

Perseus grew up and fought many monsters. He became famous for killing Medusa. Medusa was a monster with snakes for hair. Anyone who looked at Medusa turned into stone. Perseus cut off Medusa's head and gave it to the goddess Athena.

Leda

Zeus also had a child with Leda. Leda was the queen of Sparta.

Leda was bathing in a stream. Zeus made himself look like a white swan. Leda petted the swan. The swan then swam away.

Soon after, Leda laid a blue egg. Four children hatched from the egg. One of the children was Helen. Helen became famous for her beauty. Many men loved Helen because she was beautiful.

Alcmene

Alcmene was a mortal woman who refused Zeus' advances. She wanted to remain faithful to her husband. But Zeus would not give up.

One night, Zeus used his powers to make himself look like Alcmene's husband. Later, Alcmene discovered that she was pregnant. She gave birth to Heracles nine months later. Heracles was a great hero.

Aegina

Aegina was the beautiful daughter of the river god Asopus. Zeus wanted to be with Aegina. But he did not want Asopus or Hera to see him. So he turned himself into an eagle.

Zeus grabbed Aegina and flew away with her. He landed on Oenone Island. Zeus renamed the island Aegina.

Most of the gods and goddesses on Mount Olympus were the children of Zeus.

Later, Aegina gave birth to a son. The son became the king of Aegina. But there were no people for him to rule. Zeus solved this problem by turning ants into people.

Immortal Children

Zeus had relationships with goddesses too. Some of the goddesses had his children. These

children became gods and goddesses on Mount Olympus. Their names were Hermes, Hephaestus, Ares, Apollo, Dionysus, Athena, and Artemis. Only Ares and Hephaestus were Hera's children. Athena was Metis' child. Athena jumped out of Zeus' head when she was fully grown. Metis remained trapped inside Zeus. Most of Zeus' other children had titan goddesses as mothers.

The Muses were Zeus' children. These nine sisters were goddesses. They inspired people to be creative. Each Muse inspired a different art such as mathematics, music, and poetry.

The Fates were also Zeus' children. These goddesses were three sisters who knew about all people's pasts and futures.

The Fates measured people's lives with thread. One of the sisters spun a thread. The length of the thread showed whether a person would live a long life or a short life. The second sister wound up the thread. The third sister cut the thread. A person died when the Fate cut the thread.

Athena was one of Zeus' children.

Chapter Four

Stories about Zeus

Zeus had unlimited power as king of the gods. He often used his power to punish people or to change history. His actions often affected life on the earth.

Both gods and people obeyed Zeus' laws. They did not want to make him angry. Zeus punished those who disobeyed him. Prometheus received a severe punishment from Zeus.

Prometheus

Prometheus was a titan. He felt sorry for humans. He wanted to help them. So he gave humans the ability to make fire. Humans then could use fire to cook food and to keep warm.

Zeus was furious. Zeus did not want humans to use fire. He felt it made humans too powerful.

Zeus gave Prometheus a terrible punishment. Zeus was not happy that Prometheus gave humans fire.

Zeus chained Prometheus to a mountain. Every day, Zeus sent an eagle to eat Prometheus' liver. At night, the liver grew back again. Prometheus suffered from this punishment for many years. Finally, the hero Heracles set Prometheus free.

The Flood

Zeus thought people on the Earth were evil because they sacrificed their babies to the gods. Zeus became angry with people on Earth. Zeus decided to punish the whole world.

Zeus decided to send a flood to cover the Earth. He asked his brother Poseidon for help.

Prometheus found out about the plans for the flood. He wanted to save his demigod son. He told his son Deucalion to build a large chest. Deucalion built the chest and put food and water inside it. Then Deucalion and his wife, Pyrrha, got inside the chest.

Zeus caused rain to fall from the sky. Poseidon made rivers and oceans flood the

Poseidon made rivers and oceans flood the land.

land. The storm lasted nine days. The earth flooded. Only one mountain top was dry.

The chest floated on the water for weeks. Finally, it landed on the dry mountain top. Pyrrha and Deucalion were the only people who survived the flood.

Zeus saw Pyrrha and Deucalion. He knew they were good people who respected the gods. Zeus felt sorry for them. He dried up the land.

Zeus told Pyrrha and Deucalion to throw stones behind them. Pyrrha and Deucalion obeyed Zeus. The stones they threw turned into people. These people were the Stone People. They were strong people who helped rebuild the world after the flood.

The storm lasted nine days.

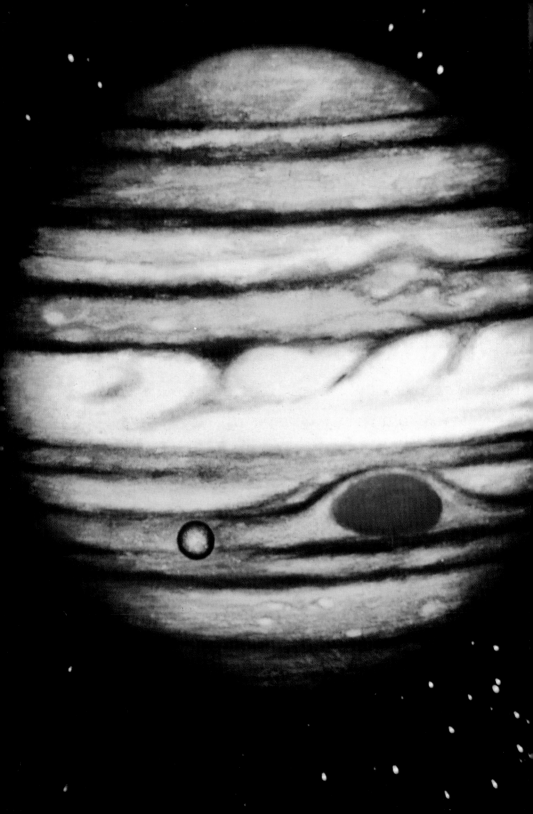

Chapter Five

Mythology in the Modern World

Characters from Greek and Roman myths have affected many areas of modern life. For example, astronomers named the planets in our solar system for characters from Roman myths. The fifth planet from the Sun is the largest planet in the solar system. Astronomers named it Jupiter after the Roman name for Zeus, the king of the gods.

Art, Architecture, and Literature

Characters in mythology are the subjects of many famous paintings and sculptures. Pictures of Zeus throwing lightning bolts decorate vases and jars.

Myths have influenced architecture. Architecture is the planning of buildings.

Astronomers named the fifth planet from the Sun Jupiter for Zeus, the king of the gods.

People often create buildings that look like ancient temples. These modern buildings may have many columns like the temples once had.

Myths are part of literature. Famous books often refer to characters or action from myths. People today still enjoy reading the myths. Students often study myths in school.

Influences on Language

Many words and definitions in use today come from mythology. For example, Zeus made the titan Atlas carry the heavens on his shoulders. Today, an atlas is a collection of maps.

The Muses also have a place in modern language. Some artists say a muse has inspired them to paint or draw.

People sometimes name geographical features after characters in classical mythology. Zeus carried Europa a great distance from Asia to Crete. People named the continent Europe for Europa to honor her long journey.

The Test of Time

The world has changed greatly since the days when Greeks and Romans told stories to

Zeus made Atlas carry the heavens on his shoulders.

explain the world. People rarely create new stories to explain the world. Instead, most people trust scientists to explain the principles of nature.

Even so, people still enjoy reading classical mythology. Adventure, love, magic, and surprise fill the pages of myths. The stories connect people today with people from another time. They help today's readers understand people who lived thousands of years ago.

Words to Know

architecture (AR-ki-tek-chur)—the planning of buildings

cyclops (SYE-clahpss)—a giant with one eye in the middle of its forehead

demigod (DE-mee-gahd)—a half-human, half-god character in mythology

immortal (i-MOR-tuhl)—having the ability to live forever

myth (MITH)—a story with a purpose; myths often describe quests or explain natural events.

nymph (NIMF)—a female goddess who lives in a forest, a meadow, a mountain, or a stream

titan (TYE-tuhn)—a powerful giant

To Learn More

Green, Robert Lancelyn. *Tales of the Greek Heroes*. New York: Puffin, 1995.

Hull, Robert. *Roman Stories*. New York: Thomson Learning, 1994.

McCaughrean, Geraldine. *Greek Myths*. New York: Margaret McElderry Publications, 1993.

Nardo, Don. *Greek and Roman Mythology*. San Diego, Calif.: Lucent Books, 1997.

Williams, Marcia. *Greek Myths for Young Children*. Cambridge, Mass.: Candlewick Press, 1995.

Useful Addresses

American Classical League
Miami University
Oxford, OH 45056-1694

American Philological Association
John Marincola, Secretary/Treasurer
19 University Place, Room 328
New York, NY 10003-4556

**Classical Association of the Middle West
    and South**
Gregory Daugherty, Secretary/Treasurer
Department of Classics
Randolph-Macon College
Ashland, VA 23005

Ontario Classical Association
2072 Madden Boulevard
Oakville, ON L6H 3L6
Canada

Internet Sites

The Book of Gods, Goddesses, Heroes, and Other Characters of Mythology
http://www.cybercomm.net/~grandpa/gdsindex.html

Encyclopedia Mythica
http://www.pantheon.org/mythica/areas

Mythology
http://www.windows.umich.edu/mythology/mythology.html

Myths and Legends
http://pubpages.unh.edu/~cbsiren/myth.html

The Perseus Project
http://www.perseus.tufts.edu/

World Mythology: Ancient Greek and Roman
http://www.artsMIA.org/mythology/ancientgreekandroman.html

Index